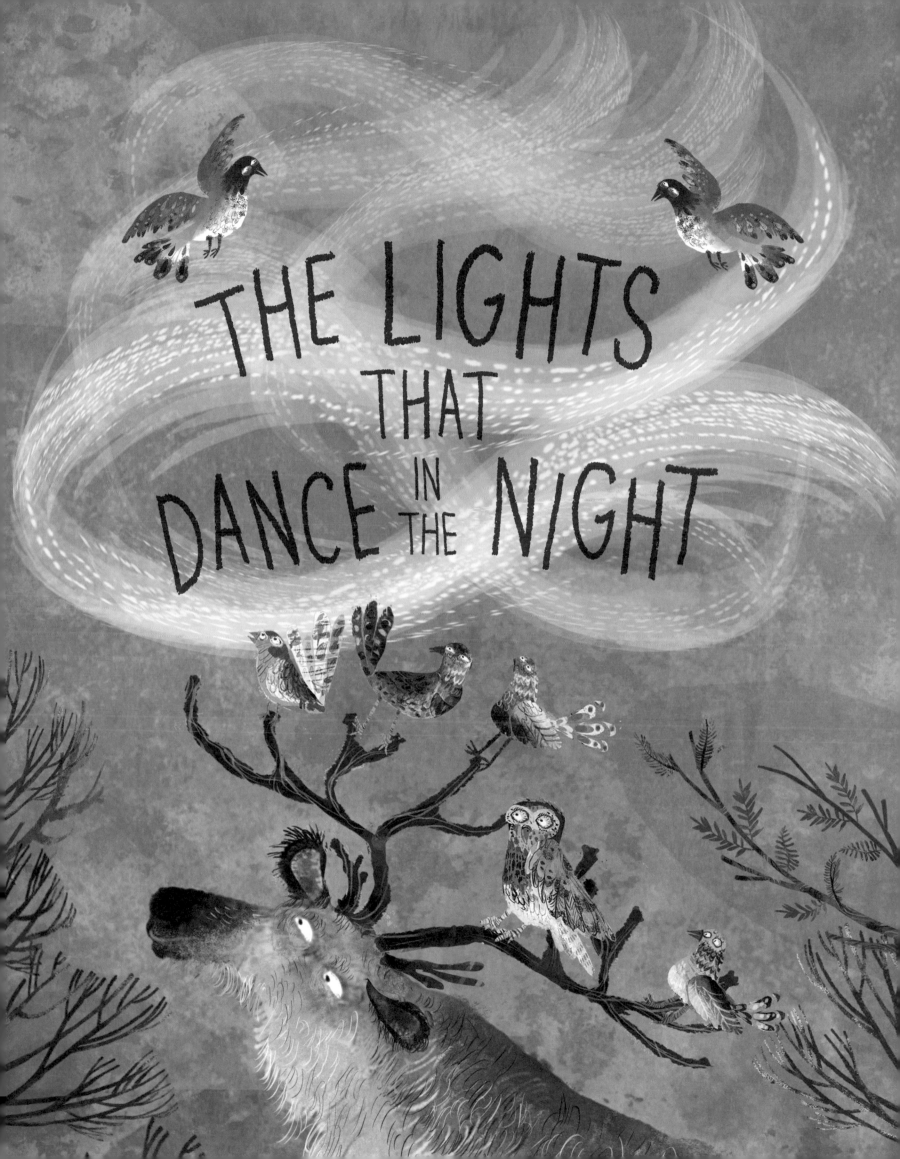

Dedicated to all
the light seekers.

OXFORD
UNIVERSITY PRESS

Great Clarendon Street, Oxford OX2 6DP

Oxford University Press is a department of the University of Oxford.
It furthers the University's objective of excellence in research, scholarship,
and education by publishing worldwide. Oxford is a registered trade mark of
Oxford University Press in the UK and in certain other countries

Text and illustrations copyright © Yuval Zommer 2021

Author photo by Ian Hessenberg

The moral rights of the author and illustrator have been asserted
Database right Oxford University Press (maker)

First published 2021

British Library Cataloguing in Publication Data
Data available

ISBN: 978-0-19-276984-8

1 3 5 7 9 10 8 6 4 2

Printed in China

Paper used in the production of this book
is a natural, recyclable product made from wood
grown in sustainable forests. The manufacturing process conforms
to the environmental regulations of the country of origin.

THE LIGHTS THAT DANCE IN THE NIGHT

YUVAL ZOMMER

OXFORD
UNIVERSITY PRESS

We are the lights
that dance in the night.

We started our journey as specks
of dust blown to Earth
from the Sun.

We tumbled through clouds, through winds and snowstorms too.

Staying strong,
keeping together,

we found a path through
wintry weather.

And then we changed,
as in a dream.
Through streams of air,
we shone. We gleamed.

We knew what we
were meant to be.

We are the lights
that dance in the night.

Our colours brought joy to polar bears,
and happiness to Arctic hares.

Flippers clapped to see us swirl . . .
and bright bills touched with every twirl.

Our dancing lights made whales sing
and bells on boats began to ring.

We sashayed for an Arctic fox.
We swayed above an old musk ox.

Wolf packs howled beneath our glow
and wild cats played on painted snow.

We lit the skies for forest birds,
we sparkled over reindeer herds.

Storytellers wove our lights
into tales for long, dark nights.

People stopped to stand and stare,
to feel the magic in the air.

Young and old,

big and small,

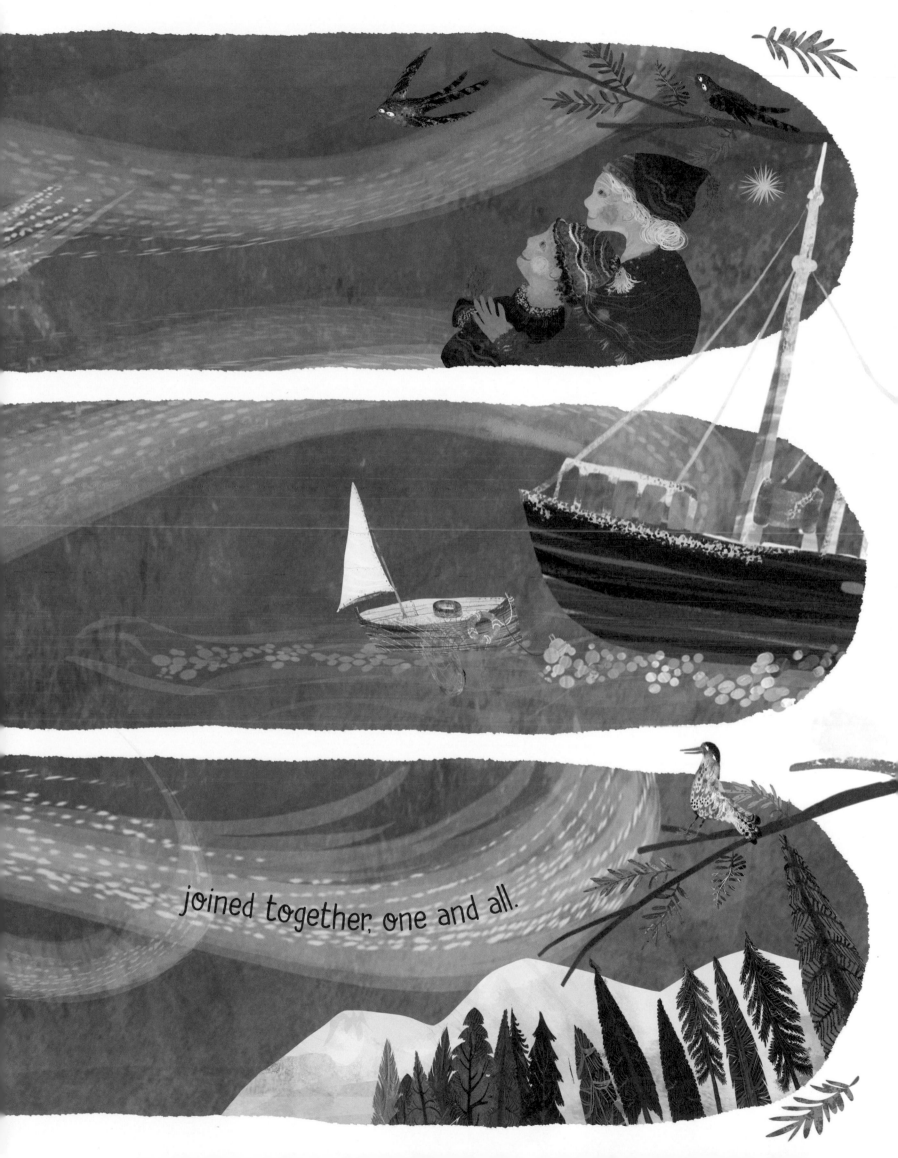

joined together, one and all.

Across this Arctic sweep of land and sea,
they raised their voices cheerfully.

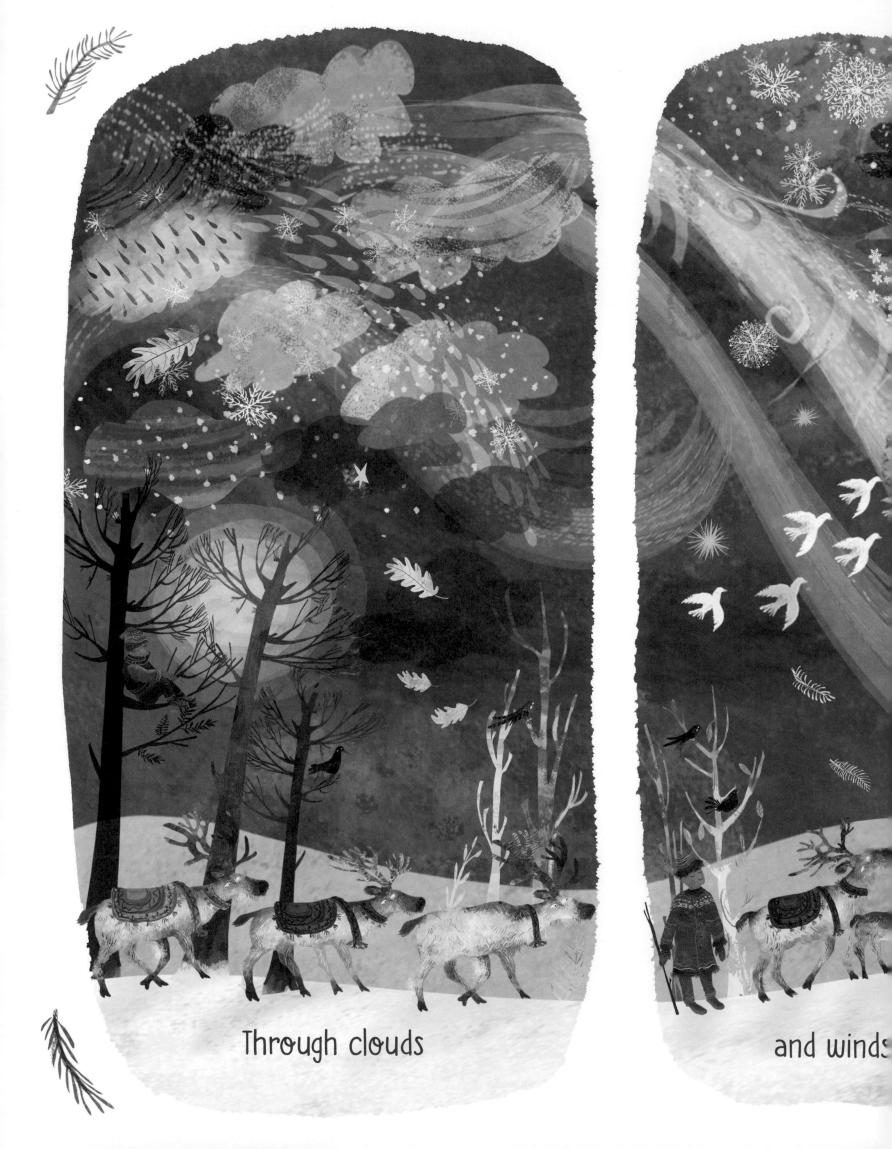

Through clouds

and winds

and storms   we came . . .

illuminating darkness,
keeping hope aflame.

A miracle of winter . . .
we are the lights
that dance in the night.